# Veteran Adventure Stories: Charlie Plumb

Stephanie Hennessy

Published by Generations of Courage Press

For permission requests, write to:
veteran.adventure.stories@gmail.com

**Image Credits:**

**Public Domain Images (via Wikimedia Commons):**
*Hỏa Lò Prison (Aerial View); F-4 on Aircraft Carrier; F-4 Over Land; F-4 Vietnam; POW Flag.*

**Charles Plumb Personal Photographs (Used with Permission):**
*Prisoner's Cup; Proof of Life; Charlie and Susan; Charlie and Family; Charlie and F-4."*

ISBN-13: 979-8-9929663-1-2

Proudly Printed in the United States of America

# *AUTHOR'S NOTE*

To Kids:

Heroes are all around you. They don't wear superhero capes, and you might not know their names. They are the men and women who rose when their nation needed them and faced down fear with bravery. Remember these heroes when you are having a hard day.

How can you be brave like them?

To Parents:

After searching to find a good veteran-themed book to read to my young son, I realized that the stories of our warriors are often relegated to adult nonfiction.

I believe it is important for children to hear these stories and to have someone real to inspire them. Whenever possible, I interview the veteran and family members when creating their life's tale. May these stories of adventure engage your children in lessons of civics, bravery, and the power of the American dream.

*Stephani Hennessy.*

Hi there. I'm Charlie.

When I was born, the whole world was in a
terrible, roaring war. But my whole world was
my family and our magical farm in Kansas.

I spent my days playing outside. My sister and I fed animals, climbed haystacks, and explored the countryside. We were always ready for an adventure.

One of our smelliest adventures was at the cow pond behind our house. Wiggly tadpoles filled the muddy water. Islands of cow poop floated on the surface. My sister dared me to jump in. "Watch out for the cow patties!" she yelled.

I wasn't sure I wanted to swim in that yucky place! I couldn't let my sister swim alone, so I had to do it.

We ran home after hours of splashing. Mom laughed as
we came in, "What happened to you two?"

She rushed us to the bath, teasing, "You brought half
the pond and almost all the cows with you!"

Dad worked in a noisy factory making weapons to help with the war. The bangs and clanks were so loud that you couldn't even think.

One day, there was a huge crash. Dad's ears wouldn't stop buzzing and ringing.

When it was time to go to war, dad wanted to do his part to protect the people he cared about.

But the doctors told him no. His hearing wasn't strong enough. Dad came home that day with low shoulders. He was quiet for a long time.

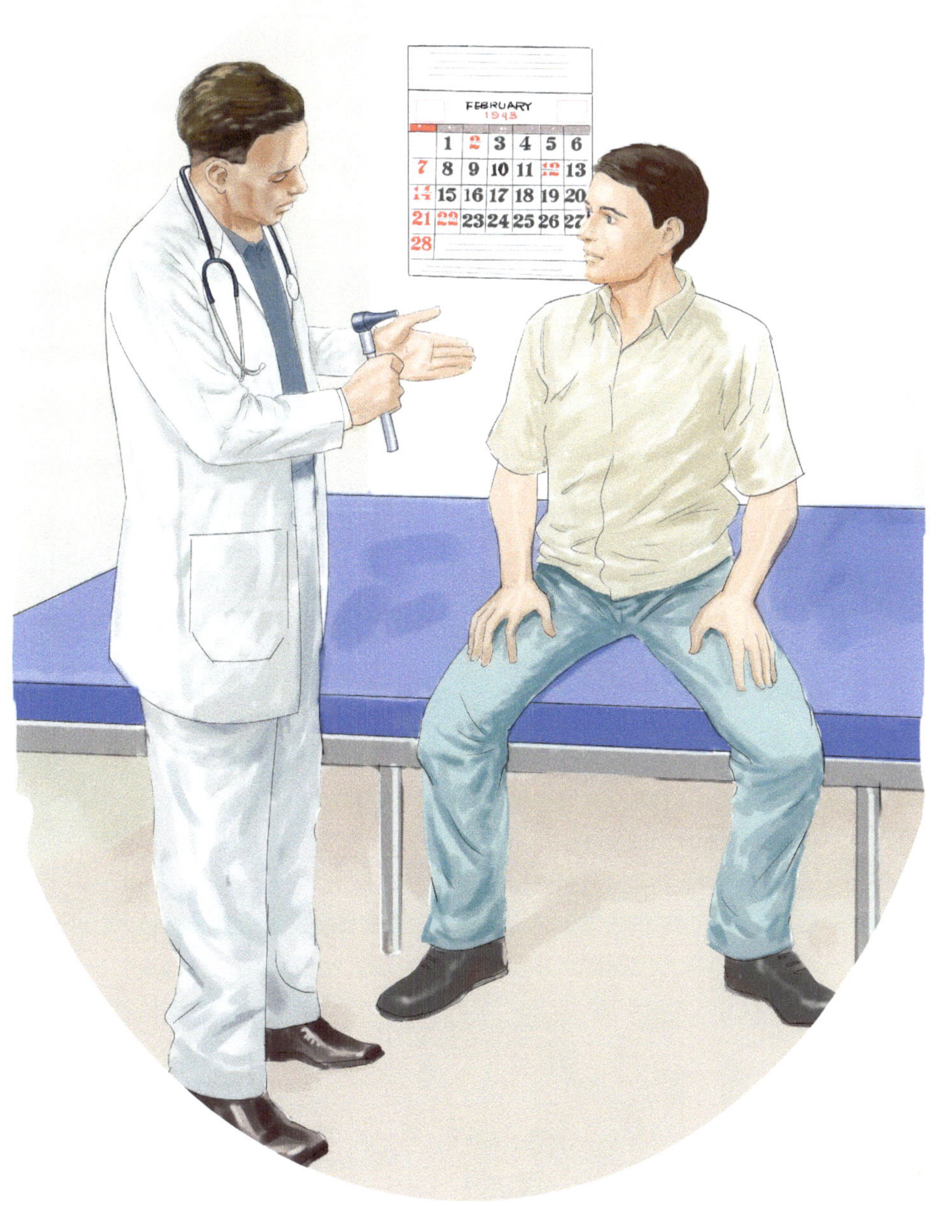

When I was thirteen, we moved to the city. I was scared to make friends. Mom told me I should try new things. I joined the scouts and learned to tie cool knots. I played trumpet in the band.

Soon enough, I had plenty of friends, and the world was a little less scary. With every passing day, I liked my new home more and more.

I dreamed of going to college, but it cost money that we didn't have. I wrote letters to anyone who might help. My hand got sore from writing so many letters!

One day, a serious-looking letter came in the mail. As I read it, I burst through the door and shouted, "Mom! You won't believe this!"

It was from the Navy college. I got in! Before college, I had only been to five states.

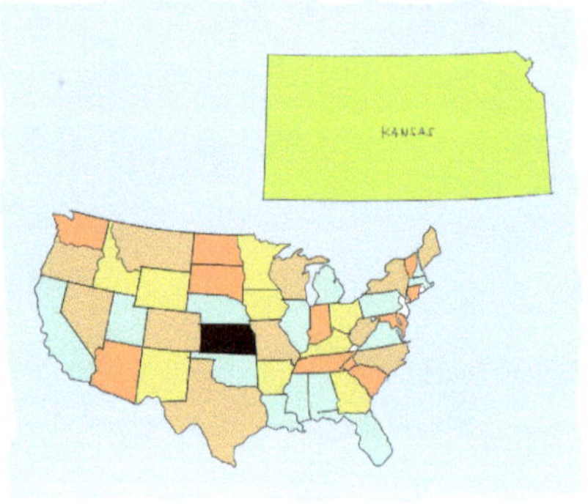

I had never seen the ocean, not even once.

I had never been on an airplane, either.

My world was about to get a lot bigger!

The Navy school had a fighter jet program. It was hard to get into. Only a few students earned a spot.

I added my name to the list with a shaking hand, feeling nervous and excited.

Announcement day came. My heart raced as I scanned the names.

There it was- I got in!

Pretty soon, I sat in the pilot's seat learning to fly a fighter jet.

I felt like an eagle soaring through the wide open skies.

After graduation, America was at war with a country called North Vietnam. My mission was to go there. When I told my mom, her smile faded.

I could see she was worried. She didn't want anything bad to happen to me.

But I was excited. I had trained for this. Like my dad, I wanted to do my part.

"Don't worry," I told her with a grin. "I'll be back by the Fourth of July!" I believed it would be over in no time, just like swimming in the cow pond.

Life on a giant ship with hundreds of other sailors felt busy at first.

Letters to my family helped me describe life on the ship.

When a letter came, it felt like a piece of my family found me.

Months went by. The other sailors became my friends.
One liked to guess who might be in danger the next day.

One night, he pointed at me and teased, "Better watch
it, Charlie! Looks like bad luck for you tomorrow!"

I tried to laugh, but his words stuck with me.

I couldn't shake the nervous feeling.

The next morning, I climbed into my fighter jet, ready
for another day in the sky. Flying high above the clouds
felt like being a bird—free and unstoppable.

Things didn't stay calm for long. Down below, enemy
soldiers spotted me.

Suddenly, the plane shook and began to fall. My heart raced as I pulled the emergency handle. I prayed for a safe landing.

I hit the ground softly. A group of enemy soldiers rushed toward me. They took me to a place called "Hotel Hanoi."

It wasn't a hotel at all. It was a hard and lonely prison.
Bugs were everywhere. We swatted mosquitoes day and
night. Our clothes were dirty and itchy, and we almost
never got to wash them.

We couldn't write home, and no mail reached us. Worst
of all, the guards yelled at us and said mean things. I
missed my family more than ever.

Americans crowded the camp. We needed to stay strong.

We did push-ups to keep our bodies strong, even when we were tired or hungry.

To keep our spirits strong, we shared prayers and stories.

The guards didn't want us
to talk to each other, but
that didn't stop us.

We invented a secret
language.

It had no words, and was
called Tap Code.

We tapped on walls, on
pipes, on anything we
could find.

When I felt scared or
alone, someone would
tap, "Stay strong," or
"I'm here for you."

Tapping gave us hope. It kept us connected, even
when we weren't allowed to speak.

As time dragged on, the other prisoners and I became like family. We shared our favorite memories. We knew everyone's phone numbers.

We made a promise: if one of us went home, we would call each other's moms to let them know their kids were safe.

To keep strong, I told myself, "I'll be home by the Fourth of July." When the Fourth of July passed, I shrugged and said, "It's OK. I'll be home by Halloween!"

I did that over and over for 66 holidays. That's a lot of birthdays, Easters, and Christmases. Each brought me a little closer to freedom.

Rescue took 2,103 long days, but we were going home at last!

After almost six years in the prison camp, I saw American skies once again.

The country held a huge parade to celebrate our return.

People cheered, waved flags, and called us heroes.

I didn't feel like a hero.

I lost my plane and hadn't finished my mission.

When people said, "Thank you for your service," I didn't know what to say back.

Everything felt different.

The world had changed while I was gone.

I had changed too.

Simple things felt weird. I sat with my family for a favorite meal, but couldn't finish my plate.

I took a walk outside by myself, but looked for guards that weren't there.

It was hard to remember how to enjoy being free.

With a lot of help and patience from people I loved, I started to feel normal again.

In my life, I've learned that even in the hardest times, faith in God keeps you moving forward.

I've learned that it is healthy to forgive those who hurt you.

I've learned that true strength comes from supporting each other, caring for others, and staying hopeful.

I always believe that in the end, good times will come.

# More About Charlie Plumb

Today, Charlie lives with his wife, Susan, in sunny California. They have four grown children and four lively grandchildren. Charlie loves taking them up in the sky, showing them the magic he first felt as a young pilot. Charlie travels all over the country, sharing his incredible adventures and the lessons he learned during his time in the Navy. He still loves flying, and so far, he hasn't had to use his parachute again for an emergency landing.

To learn more about Charlie's story, please visit:
**www.charlieplumb.com**

*Photos Courtesy of Charles Plumb*

# WHAT IS A
# PRISONER OF WAR?

A Prisoner of War (POW) is a member of the military who is captured during war. They are not allowed to go home.

The POW Flag

POWs cannot talk to their families, and they do not have many clothes, food, or clean water. But even in hard places, POWs have stayed brave by helping each other. They share stories and help each other never give up hope.

Charlie's "Proof of Life" Photo

Charlie Plumb was a POW held in Hoa Lo Prison, which came to be called "Hotel Hanoi." In 1973, 591 Americans were released from North Vietnamese POW camps.

Charlie used this cup to tap, eat, and drink.

Aerial view of Hỏa Lò Prison.

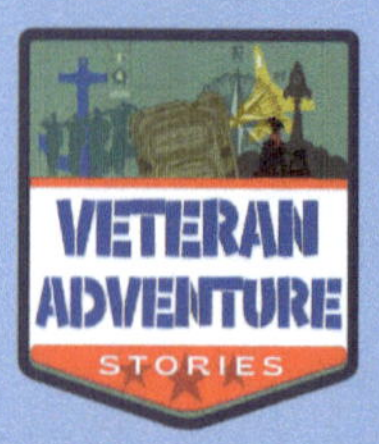



# BEING BRAVE

## What does it mean to be brave?

Brave people feel scared too. Being brave doesn't mean you are fearless. It means you feel scared, but choose to keep trying anyway.

## Charlie's Bravery

He tried new things.

He helped others.

He never gave up hope.

He remembered the people he loved.

## Your Bravery Checklist

- ☐ Try something new.
- ☐ Help a friend.
- ☐ Say something kind.
- ☐ Keep going when something is hard.
- ☐ Take a deep breath when you're worried.

## Your Brave Pose

Stand tall like Charlie.

Put your shoulders back, lift your chin, and take a breath.

**How does your brave pose make you feel?**

## Reflection

What is one brave thing you want to try this week?

# CHARLIE PLUMB

## Vocabulary Check

Vietnam– A country in Asia where Charlie flew missions.
Parachute– A cloth that opens to help someone float safely down.
Capture– To be taken and not allowed to leave.
Resilience– To keep going, even when life is hard.
Courage– Being brave, even when you feel scared.
Code– A secret way of sending messages, like Tap Code.

## Tap Code

At Hotel Hanoi, prisoners used a secret way to talk. It let them send messages without any words at all.

Step 1: Tap down to show the row.
Step 2: Tap across to show the column.
Let's try the word COW:

| TAPS | 1 | 2 | 3 | 4 | 5 |
|------|---|---|---|---|---|
| 1 | A | B | C | D | E |
| 2 | F | G | H | I | J |
| 3 | L | M | N | O | P |
| 4 | Q | R | S | T | U |
| 5 | V | W | X | Y | Z |

- C = one tap, pause, then three taps.
- O = three taps, pause, then four taps.
- W = five taps, pause, then two taps.

So COW looks like this:

• | ••• || ••• | •••• || ••••• | •• ||

Now you try! Can you figure out this word?

•• | ••• || • | ••••• || •••• | •• || ••• | ••••

### What about you?

- What is something you worked hard to learn?
- What helps you stay strong when life feels hard?
- Who is your hero?

### What happened first?

_____ Charlie spent almost six years in Hotel Hanoi.

_____ Charlie and his sister played on a farm.

_____ Charlie was rescued and returned home.

_____ Charlie used Tap Code to stay strong.

_____ Charlie parachuted to the ground.

# THE F-4 PHANTOM II

**1** It took off from huge aircraft carriers. Charlie flew from the USS *Coral Sea* and USS *Kitty Hawk*.



**2** The Phantom was famous for its roar. Some people said it sounded angry—like a roaring dragon!

**3** The F-4 could fly over 1,400 miles per hour. That's almost twice the speed of sound!

**4** It protected other planes. F-4s guarded slower aircraft and kept them safe from enemy fighters.

**5** The Phantom carried two people. One flew the jet, and the second worked the radar and weapons. Charlie sat in the front seat.

Image credits: Public domain images via Wikimedia Commons.

## Try This!

What would you name a jet that flies faster than sound?

www.ingramcontent.com/pod-product-compliance
Lightning Source LLC
Chambersburg PA
CBHW061031100726
47911CB00001B/38